MACMILLAN GUIDED READERS

ELEMENTARY LEVEL

SIR ARTHUR CONAN DOYLE

The Hound of the Baskervilles

Retold by Stephen Colbourn

MACMILLAN
CLASSICS

ELEMENTARY LEVEL

Founding Editor: John Milne

Macmillan Guided Readers provide a choice of enjoyable reading material for all learners of English. The series comprises three categories: MODERNS, CLASSICS and ORIGINALS. Macmillan **Classics** are retold versions of internationally recognised literature, published at four levels of grading – Beginner, Elementary, Intermediate and Upper. At **Elementary Level**, the control of content and language has the following main features:

Information Control
Stories have straightforward plots and a restricted number of main characters. Information which is vital to the understanding of the story is clearly presented and repeated when necessary. Difficult allusion and metaphor are avoided and cultural backgrounds are made explicit.

Structure Control
Students will meet those grammatical features which they have already been taught in their elementary course of studies. Other grammatical features occasionally occur with which the students may not be so familiar, but their use is made clear through context and reinforcement. This ensures that the reading as well as being enjoyable provides a continual learning situation for the students. Sentences are kept short – a maximum of two clauses in nearly all cases – and within sentences there is a balance of simple adverbial and adjectival phrases. Great care is taken with pronoun reference.

Vocabulary Control
At **Elementary Level** there is a limited use of carefully controlled vocabulary of approximately 1100 basic words. At the same time, students are given some opportunity to meet new or unfamiliar words in contexts where their meaning is obvious. The meaning of words introduced in this way is reinforced by repetition. Help is also given to the students in the form of vivid illustrations which are closely related to the text.

Contents

A Note about This Story

This story was written by Sir Arthur Conan Doyle. It is an adventure about a detective called Sherlock Holmes. A friend of Sherlock Holmes, Dr Watson, tells the story.

Sherlock Holmes is not a policeman. He is a private detective. People pay him to find things that are lost or stolen. Holmes also solves mysteries and catches criminals.

This story takes place in 1889. There were no telephones at this time. If someone wanted to send an important message quickly, they sent a telegram.

The Hound of the Baskervilles takes place in the southwest of England on Dartmoor. Dartmoor is a wild and lonely place. Not many people live there. Dartmoor can be a dangerous place to live too.

On Dartmoor there are many high, rocky hills. These hills are called tors. There are also pieces of land called mires. These are areas of soft, very deep mud with grass growing on top. Men and animals who fall into the mires can die.

The People in This Story

Sherlock Holmes is a very clever detective. He lives and works in London at 221B Baker Street.

Dr Watson is Sherlock Holmes' friend. He helps Sherlock Holmes to solve mysteries.

Dr Mortimer lives near Dartmoor in the south-west of England. He is a doctor of medicine.

Sir Hugo Baskerville was the owner of Baskerville Hall in 1645.

Sir Charles Baskerville was the owner of Baskerville Hall at the beginning of this story. Dr Mortimer thinks Sir Charles was murdered.

Sir Henry Baskerville is the new owner of Baskerville Hall. He has come from Canada to live in England.

Mr and Mrs Barrymore are servants at Baskerville Hall.

Mr Jack Stapleton lives in Merripit House near Grimpen Mire. Stapleton is interested in the plants, birds and insects on Dartmoor.

7

Miss Stapleton is Jack Stapleton's sister. She lives in Merripit House. She is a tall, beautiful woman with dark hair and dark eyes.

Mr Frankland lives in Lafter Hall near Coombe Tracey. He is interested in studying the stars and has a large telescope.

Selden is an escaped prisoner from Dartmoor Prison.

1

Mr Sherlock Holmes

My name is Doctor Watson. I am writing this story about my friend, Mr Sherlock Holmes, the famous detective.

Sherlock Holmes lives at 221B Baker Street, in the middle of London. My story begins in Baker Street, one morning in 1889, when a man knocked on the door.

I heard the man say, 'Mr Holmes? My name is Dr Mortimer. I need your help.'

'Come in,' said Holmes. 'How can I help you?'

'I have a strange story to tell you, Mr Holmes,' said Dr Mortimer. 'My story is very strange. Perhaps you will not believe me.'

2

The Curse of the Baskervilles

Dr Mortimer sat down. Sherlock Holmes and I listened to his story.

'I am a doctor and I work in the country,' said Dr Mortimer. 'I live and work on Dartmoor. And, as you know, Dartmoor is a large, wild place. There is only one big house on Dartmoor – Baskerville Hall. The owner of the house was Sir Charles Baskerville. I was his friend as well as his doctor.'

'I read of his death in *The Times* newspaper,' said Holmes.

'That was three months ago,' said Dr Mortimer. 'The newspaper reported his death, but it did not report all the facts.'

'Was there something strange about his death?' asked Sherlock Holmes.

'I am not certain,' said Dr Mortimer. 'There was a story about a curse on the Baskerville family. Sir Charles believed this old story.'

'A curse?' I asked. 'What do you mean?'

'Here is the story,' said Dr Mortimer. He took a large piece of paper out of his pocket. 'Please read this. It is the story of the Curse of the Baskervilles.'

Holmes took the paper and read it. 'It is called *The Hound of the Baskervilles*,' he said. He showed me the paper. This is what it said:

In the year 1645, Sir Hugo Baskerville was the owner of Baskerville Hall. Sir Hugo was a cruel man who did not believe in God. Every day he went out hunting and drinking with a gang of wild friends.

A farmer on Dartmoor had a beautiful daughter. Sir Hugo wanted to marry the girl, but she was afraid of him. The girl's father told Sir Hugo to stay away from his farm. Sir Hugo was very angry.

One day, when the farmer was working in his fields, Sir Hugo rode to the farm with his friends. They caught the girl and took her to Baskerville Hall.

The poor girl was terrified. Sir Hugo locked her in a bedroom. Then he started drinking with his gang. When he was drunk, he became more wild and cruel. He shouted at his men and hit them.

The frightened girl waited until it was dark. Then she opened a window and escaped from Baskerville Hall.

10

'Please read this. It is the story of the *Curse* of the
Baskervilles.'

Her father's farm was about four miles away. It was night, but she was able to follow the path in the moonlight. She started to run across the dark moor.

Sir Hugo went to the girl's room. It was empty and Sir Hugo was terribly angry. He ran to his men and jumped onto the table where they were drinking. He kicked the plates and glasses off the table. 'Fetch the horses!' he shouted. 'Get the girl!'

They all ran outside and jumped onto their horses. Sir Hugo kept a pack of wild dogs for hunting. 'Let the dogs find her!' he shouted. 'The Devil can take me if I do not catch her!'

The dogs ran out across the dark moor. Sir Hugo and his men rode after them. The dogs barked and Sir Hugo shouted.

Then they heard another noise. It was louder than the noise of barking and shouting. The dogs stopped and listened. They were afraid.

The men heard the noise too. It was a loud and deep howling sound – the sound of a huge dog howling at the moon. The men stopped their horses, but Sir Hugo rode on. He wanted to catch the girl.

Sir Hugo did not catch the girl. Suddenly his horse stopped and threw him to the ground. The horse ran away in terror.

In the moonlight, the men saw a strange, black animal. It looked liked a dog with huge, fiery eyes. But it was as big as a horse. All the men became very frightened.

The huge black dog jumped on Sir Hugo Baskerville and killed him. The other men ran away into the night and Sir Hugo was never seen again.

Since that time, many of the sons of the Baskerville family have died while they were young. Many of them have died strangely. This is the Curse of the Baskervilles. The black dog – The Hound of the Baskervilles – still walks on the moor at night.

'Well, Mr Holmes, what do you think of this story?' asked Dr Mortimer.

'I do not think it is a true story,' said Sherlock Holmes. 'Why do you show me this story? Do you believe it?'

'Before Sir Charles Baskerville's death, I did not believe the story,' Dr Mortimer answered. 'But Sir Charles believed the story. It worried him. He became ill and his heart was weak.'

'Why did he believe this story?' I asked.

'Because he saw the hound on the moor,' answered Dr Mortimer. 'Or, he thought he saw it. When Sir Charles told me this story, I told him to take a holiday. I told him to go to London for a few weeks and forget all about the curse.'

'Did he take a holiday?' I asked.

'No,' said Dr Mortimer. 'He planned to go to London the following Friday. But, on the Thursday evening, he went for a walk on the edge of the moor. And he never returned.'

'How did he die?' I asked.

'He died of a heart attack,' answered Dr Mortimer. 'His servant came to fetch me. I found Sir Charles near the house, on the edge of the moor. He was running away from something when he died. I am sure of that. I think he was terrified of something.'

'Terrified?' asked Holmes. 'What was he running away from?'

'I looked at the ground where Sir Charles had walked. I saw his footprints,' said Dr Mortimer. 'But there were other footprints on the ground. They were not the footprints of a man. They were the footprints of a gigantic hound!'

3

The Problem

Holmes and I were surprised. This was a very strange story. I did not believe that Sir Charles Baskerville had been killed by a gigantic black dog. But I wanted to know the truth.

'Who else saw these footprints?' asked Sherlock Holmes. His bright eyes shone and he leant forward in his chair.

'No one else saw the footprints,' answered Dr Mortimer. 'There was a lot of rain in the night. By morning, the footprints had been washed away.'

'How large were the footprints? Were they larger than the footprints of a sheepdog?'

'Yes, Mr Holmes, much larger. They were not the prints of an ordinary dog.'

'Also, you say that Sir Charles ran away from this dog? How do you know?' asked Holmes.

'The ground was soft,' answered Dr Mortimer. 'I saw Sir Charles' footprints outside Baskerville Hall. His footprints were close together as he walked along a path at the edge of the moor. Then he stopped and waited by a wooden gate. After that his footprints changed – they became wide apart and deep. I am sure he began to run. He ran towards the house. I believe that something came from the moor. I believe he saw the Hound of the Baskervilles.'

'Yes, yes,' said Holmes, 'but how do you know that Sir Charles waited by this wooden gate?'

'Because he smoked a cigar,' said Dr Mortimer. 'I saw the white cigar ash on the ground.'

'Good,' said Holmes, 'good – you are a detective.'

'Thank you,' said Dr Mortimer, with a smile.

'But you believe that Sir Charles was killed by a gigantic hound?'

'I know he ran away from something,' said Dr Mortimer. 'I know I saw those strange footprints of a huge dog. But . . .' He looked at his watch. '. . . I am meeting Sir Henry Baskerville at Waterloo Station in an hour. Sir Henry is Sir Charles' nephew. He has come from Canada. Sir Charles had no children, so Sir Henry is now the owner of Baskerville Hall. And now I have a problem.'

'What is your problem?' asked Holmes.

'I believe that Sir Henry is in danger,' said Dr Mortimer. 'Is it safe to take him to Baskerville Hall?'

'I must think,' said Sherlock Holmes. 'Stay in London tonight. Come and see me again tomorrow morning. Please bring Sir Henry with you.'

'I shall do so,' said Dr Mortimer. He stood up. 'Now I must go to meet Sir Henry at Waterloo Station. Good day.'

When Dr Mortimer had left, Holmes said to me, 'We have a problem here, Watson. There are three questions. What is the crime? Who did it? How was it done?'

'I believe he saw the Hound of the Baskervilles.'

Sir Henry Baskerville

The next morning, Dr Mortimer brought Sir Henry Baskerville to Baker Street. Sir Henry was about thirty years old. He was not tall, but he was broad and strong. He looked like a boxer.

'How do you do, Mr Holmes,' said Sir Henry. 'I arrived in London yesterday and two strange things have happened already.'

'Please sit down, Sir Henry,' said Holmes. 'Tell me what has happened.'

'No one knows that I am staying at the Northumberland Hotel,' said Sir Henry. 'But I have received a letter. Here is the letter. You see, the words are cut from a newspaper except for the word "moor".'

'The words are cut from *The Times* newspaper,' said Holmes.

'But how did this person know where I am staying?' asked Sir Henry.

'I do not know,' said Holmes. 'But you said that two strange things have happened. What is the other strange thing?'

'I have lost a boot,' said Sir Henry. 'Someone has stolen one of my boots at the hotel.'

'One of your boots?' asked Holmes. 'Someone took only one?'

'Yes,' answered Sir Henry. 'The boots are new. I bought them yesterday and I have never worn them. But why take only one?'

'That is a very good question,' said Holmes. 'I would like to visit your hotel. Perhaps I shall find the answer.'

'Then, please join us for lunch,' said Sir Henry. 'Now, if you will excuse me, I have some other business. Shall we meet at two o'clock for lunch at the Northumberland Hotel?'

'We shall come at two,' said Holmes.

Sir Henry Baskerville and Dr Mortimer left the house and walked along Baker Street. Sherlock Holmes watched them through the window of his study.

'Quick, Watson, we must follow them,' said Holmes.

I put on my hat and followed Holmes into the street. 'Why are we following them?' I asked in surprise.

'Because, my dear Watson, someone else is also following them,' said Holmes. 'Look! There is the man. There in that cab!'

I looked where Holmes was pointing. A horse-drawn cab was moving slowly along the street. A man with a black beard was sitting in the cab. He was watching Sir Henry and Dr Mortimer as they walked towards Oxford Street.

A man with a black beard was sitting in the cab.
He was watching Sir Henry and Dr Mortimer.

The man with the black beard turned round as Holmes pointed at him. He saw us and shouted to the cab driver, 'Drive! Drive quickly!' The cab driver whipped the horse and the cab disappeared round a corner.

'I think we have the answer to one of our questions,' said Holmes. 'That man with the black beard followed Sir Henry to the Northumberland Hotel. He is the man who sent the letter.'

5

The Stolen Boot

We arrived at the Northumberland Hotel at ten minutes to two. Sir Henry Baskerville was talking to the hotel manager.

'Two boots in two days,' Sir Henry said loudly. 'Two boots have disappeared from my room – one new boot and one old boot.'

'We shall look everywhere, sir,' said the manager. 'We shall find your stolen boots.'

Sir Henry was silent while we ate lunch. He was angry about his stolen boots.

'Tell me, Mr Holmes,' said Dr Mortimer. 'Is it safe for Sir Henry to go to Baskerville Hall?'

'It is safer than staying in London,' said Holmes. 'Do you know that a man followed you this morning?'

'Followed us!' said Dr Mortimer in surprise. 'Who followed us?'

'A man with a thick black beard,' said Holmes. 'Do you know a man with a black beard?'

'Yes, I do,' replied Dr Mortimer. 'The servant at Baskerville Hall has a thick black beard. His name is Barrymore. I can't think why he is following us. But I am sure Sir Henry is in danger. It is better if Sir Henry stays here in London.'

'No. You are wrong,' said Holmes. 'There are millions of people in London. We cannot watch them all. There are not as many people on Dartmoor. Everyone will notice someone who is a stranger.'

'But this man may not be a stranger,' said Dr Mortimer.

'I agree,' said Holmes. 'That is why Sir Henry must not stay at Baskerville Hall alone. I myself will be busy in London, but my good friend Dr Watson will go with you to Dartmoor.'

'Oh . . . yes, of course,' I said, 'I will certainly go to Dartmoor.'

'Thank you, Dr Watson,' said Sir Henry. 'You will be very welcome at Baskerville Hall.'

'Good,' said Holmes. 'Now, Sir Henry, tell me about the other boot which has been stolen.'

'It is one of an old pair of boots,' said Sir Henry.

'How strange,' said Holmes. 'And, tell me Sir Henry, if you die, who will become the owner of Baskerville Hall?'

'I don't know,' replied Sir Henry. 'Sir Charles had two brothers – my father, who went to Canada, and a younger brother called Roger. But Roger never married and he died in South America. I have no living relatives. I don't know who will get all my money if I die today.'

'And, may I ask, how much money do you have?'

'Certainly, Mr Holmes. Sir Charles left me a fortune of one million pounds,' said Sir Henry.

'Many men will murder their best friend for a million pounds,' said Holmes.

6

Baskerville Hall

On Saturday morning, Sherlock Holmes came with me to Paddington Station.

'This is a dangerous business, Watson,' he said. 'Stay near to Sir Henry. Do not let him walk on the moor alone at night.'

'Don't worry, Holmes,' I said. 'I have brought my army revolver.'

'Good,' said Holmes. 'Write to me every day. Tell me what you see and hear. Tell me all the facts – everything.'

I said goodbye to Sherlock Holmes and met Sir Henry Baskerville and Dr Mortimer at the station. The train journey to Devon took three hours. We looked out of the windows at the green countryside. At last, we reached Dartmoor. Then the countryside changed from green to grey and we saw broken hills of black rock.

We got off the train at the small station in Grimpen Village. A driver was waiting with a carriage and horses to take us to Baskerville Hall. As we rode along the narrow country road, I saw a soldier on a horse. The soldier was carrying a gun and was watching the road.

I spoke to the driver. 'Why is that soldier guarding the road? Is there some trouble?'

'Why is that soldier guarding the road? Is there some trouble?'
'Yes, sir,' the driver replied.

'Yes, sir,' the driver replied. 'A prisoner has escaped from Dartmoor Prison. He's a very dangerous man. His name is Selden. He is a dangerous murderer.'

I looked across the empty moor. A cold wind blew and made me shiver. Holmes believed that someone wanted to murder Sir Henry Baskerville. Now, another murderer was out on the moor. I felt that this lonely place was very dangerous. I wanted to go back to London.

There were thick trees all round Baskerville Hall. It looked like a castle. It stood alone on the empty moor.

We stopped outside Baskerville Hall. 'I must leave you here,' said Dr Mortimer. 'I have a lot of work to do. And my wife is waiting for me at home.'

'I hope you will come to dinner very soon,' said Sir Henry.

'I will,' said Dr Mortimer. 'And if you ever need me, send for me at any time – day or night.' Then Dr Mortimer rode away in the carriage.

A man with a thick black beard and a pale face came out of the house. He greeted Sir Henry.

'Welcome to Baskerville Hall, sir. I am Barrymore. I have been a servant here for many years. My wife and I have prepared the house for you. Shall I show you around the house?'

'Yes please, Barrymore,' said Sir Henry. 'This is Dr Watson. He will be my guest for a few days.'

'Very good, sir,' said Barrymore. He took our cases into the house.

I looked carefully at Barrymore. Was he the man with a black beard who had followed Sir Henry in London? I was not sure.

Mr and Mrs Barrymore had looked after the house well.

24

Everything was in order. But the house was a cold and lonely place. There was trouble here.

That night I wrote a letter to Sherlock Holmes. I told him all that I had seen and heard. While I was writing, I heard a sound – a woman crying. The only woman in the house was Mrs Barrymore. I wondered why she was so unhappy.

7

The Stapletons of Merripit House

At breakfast next morning, I asked Sir Henry, 'Did you hear a woman crying in the night?'

'I heard a sound like crying,' said Sir Henry. 'But I thought it was the wind on the moor.'

Sir Henry had many papers to read. I left him sitting at his desk and went for a walk on the moor.

I walked for two or three miles across the empty moor. Then, behind me, I heard a voice call, 'Dr Watson!' I looked round. I thought it was Dr Mortimer. But I saw a stranger walking towards me.

'My name is Stapleton,' said the man. 'How do you do, Dr Watson. I saw Dr Mortimer this morning and he told me your name. I have heard about you. You are the friend of the famous detective, Sherlock Holmes, aren't you?'

'Yes, Mr Stapleton, I am,' I said.

'And is Mr Holmes staying at Baskerville Hall too?' asked Stapleton. 'Is he interested in Dartmoor?'

'Mr Holmes is in London,' I said. 'He is a busy man.'

'Of course,' said Stapleton. 'Please come and see my

house. It's very near here. I live with my sister.'

Stapleton led me along a narrow path across a wide, flat part of the moor. The land around us was a strange, green colour. We walked towards a hill of grey rock.

'Be very careful, Dr Watson,' said Stapleton. 'Stay on the path. We are in the Great Grimpen Mire. There is a sea of soft mud underneath the grass. If you fall in, you will never get out again.'

'Thank you for telling me,' I said. 'But why do you live here? It is a dangerous and lonely place.'

'I am a naturalist. I study nature,' said Stapleton. 'There are many interesting flowers and birds on the Great Grimpen Mire. And there are some unusual animals on Dartmoor.'

At that moment we heard a strange sound. It was a deep howling sound – the sound of a large dog. It came from some distance away.

'Stapleton! Is that the sound of a dog?' I asked.

'It is only the sound of the wind,' said Stapleton. 'The wind blows through the rocks and makes strange sounds. But here is my house – Merripit House on the moor.' He pointed to the long, low farmhouse which we could see near the hill. 'And my sister is coming to meet us.'

Miss Stapleton was a very attractive woman. She was slim and tall, with beautiful dark eyes. I thought she looked very different from her brother. She had dark hair, but her brother had fair hair. They were both about thirty years old. Stapleton looked a little older. He was a small, thin, clean-shaven man, with a long face.

'How do you do, Miss Stapleton,' I said. 'Your brother has told me about the Great Grimpen Mire and the unusual flowers and birds. Did you hear that strange sound a moment ago? Does the wind often make this sound?'

I thought Miss Stapleton looked very different from her brother.

'I heard nothing,' Miss Stapleton said quickly. She looked at her brother and I saw fear in her eyes.

Her brother looked at her angrily. 'Let us show Dr Watson our house,' he said.

I stayed for a short time. Stapleton showed me his collection of flowers and butterflies.

'I will come to Baskerville Hall to visit Sir Henry this afternoon,' said Stapleton. 'Will you tell him?'

'Of course,' I replied. 'Now, if you will excuse me, I must go back to Baskerville Hall. I hope to see you again soon.'

'Stay on the path,' said Stapleton. 'Remember the Great Grimpen Mire. Many men have died in it.'

Miss Stapleton walked outside with me. She spoke quickly, in a quiet voice. 'Dr Watson, I want to tell you about the strange sound you heard. The people here say that it is the sound of the Hound of the Baskervilles. They say it killed Sir Charles and now it will kill Sir Henry. But, please, do not tell my brother that I spoke to you. Now, go back to London. Go back today!'

She went into the house quickly. I walked along the narrow path slowly, thinking about what she had said.

8

Dr Watson's First Report

Baskerville Hall
Dartmoor

13 October 1889

My Dear Holmes,

I wrote and told you about Baskerville Hall and the people who live here. Now I have more facts to tell you. First, I will draw a map of the area. It will help you to understand my story.

Baskerville Hall is about two miles south-west of Grimpen Village. I walk to the village to post letters.

There are trees all round the Hall and a long avenue leads to a small summer-house in the garden. Sir Charles Baskerville died near the summer-house. I have marked the gate on the map. It is where Sir Charles stood and smoked a cigar. The gate opens onto the moor.

I have told you about the neighbours. Dr Mortimer lives nearby, about half-way between the villages of Grimpen and Coombe Tracey.

I have met the Stapletons. Their house is about three miles from the Hall. It is on the other side of High Tor.

There is one man I have not met. But Dr Mortimer has told me about him. His name is Mr Frankland and he lives at Lafter Hall. He has a large telescope and is interested in astronomy. He uses his telescope to look at the stars.

In the past few days, he has not looked at the stars. He has looked at the moor. He is watching the moor because the police have not caught the murderer, Selden. Mr Frankland

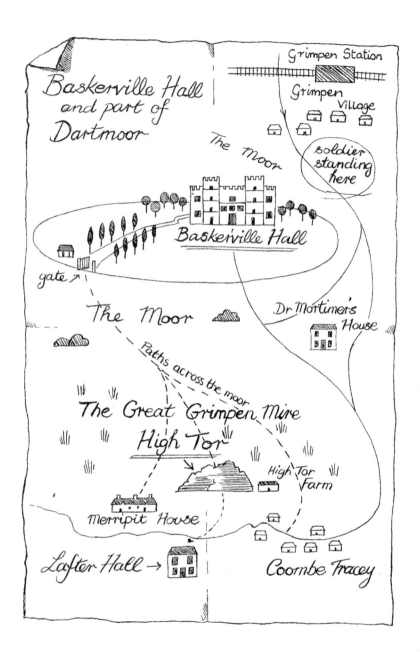

Baskerville Hall and part of Dartmoor

Grimpen Station

Grimpen Village

soldier standing here

The Moor

Baskerville Hall

gate

The Moor

Dr Mortimer's House

Paths across the moor

The Great Grimpen Mire

High Tor

High Tor Farm

Merripit House

Lafter Hall →

Coombe Tracey

watches the moor looking for strangers. But I do not think that Selden is hiding on the moor. There is no food and the weather is now very cold.

Sir Henry is worried about the Stapletons. He thinks that the murderer may break into their house. He has visited Miss Stapleton several times and they have become good friends. But Mr Stapleton is a strange man. He does not like Sir Henry visiting his sister.

Now, here is some news about Barrymore, the servant at Baskerville Hall. He looks like the man we saw in the carriage in London. You remember – the man who followed Sir Henry and Dr Mortimer to Baker Street. I told Sir Henry what I thought and he called Barrymore and asked him, 'Have you been to London recently?'

Barrymore says he has never been to London in his life Also, Sir Henry's question made him angry. He said he wanted to leave Baskerville Hall.

Sir Henry said he was sorry. He gave Barrymore some clothes and Barrymore was pleased. Barrymore and his wife thanked Sir Henry very much for the clothes.

Then, last night, I saw something very strange. In the middle of the night I heard footsteps and I looked out of my bedroom door. I saw Barrymore with a candle. I saw him walk to the end of the corridor. He stopped at the large window which looks out over the moor. He held the candle to the window and moved it backwards and forwards.

I went to the window of my own room and looked out across the moor. I saw a light moving backwards and forwards. It was somewhere near High Tor and it was clearly a signal. But a signal for what?

9

The Light On The Moor

Baskerville Hall
Dartmoor

15 October 1889

My Dear Holmes,

I am now able to answer the question at the end of my last letter. I know why Barrymore signalled with a candle.

First, let me tell you about Sir Henry and Miss Stapleton. I told you that they are very friendly. I have found out that Sir Henry is in love with her. The truth is he wants to marry her.

Yesterday morning he said to me, 'I am going to see Miss Stapleton. I want to go alone.'

'But Mr Holmes told me to stay with you,' I said. 'You must not go across the moor on your own.'

'I shall go alone,' said Sir Henry, and he went out.

I did not know what to do. I waited for ten minutes, then I decided to follow him. I did not see everything, but this is what happened.

Sir Henry met Miss Stapleton on the moor. He asked her to marry him – he told me this afterwards. They walked towards Merripit House to see Mr Stapleton. They met him outside the house. Sir Henry told Stapleton the news.

I reached High Tor before Sir Henry met Stapleton, so I saw what happened next. I saw Sir Henry talking to Stapleton. Suddenly Stapleton became wild and angry. He shouted at Sir Henry. Then he took his sister's hand and pulled her towards Merripit House.

Sir Henry turned away and walked back towards the Hall. He saw me by High Tor. He was not angry that I had followed him.

'Watson,' he said, 'that man is mad. I told him that I want to marry his sister. He shouted at me. He told me never to see her again. I think he is mad.'

I said nothing and we walked back to the Hall. That afternoon, Stapleton came to the Hall. He wanted to speak to Sir Henry. He kept saying, 'I am sorry. I was very rude.' Then he invited Sir Henry to dinner at Merripit House on Friday night.

Now I will tell you the story of Barrymore. I told Sir Henry that I had seen Barrymore signal with a candle. Sir Henry said, 'We will wait for him tonight. If he signals again, we will catch him.'

Sir Henry and I did not go to bed. We sat waiting in Sir Henry's study until two o'clock in the morning. Then we heard footsteps outside the study. We listened. The footsteps went upstairs.

Sir Henry and I waited for two more minutes. Then we opened the door quietly, and went upstairs. We saw Barrymore by the large window at the end of the corridor. He had a candle in his hand and he was waving the candle in front of the window.

'What are you doing, Barrymore?' Sir Henry shouted.

Barrymore almost dropped the candle. He looked frightened. 'Nothing, Sir Henry,' he said. 'I'm checking the window, that's all.'

'You are signalling to someone on the moor,' said Sir Henry. 'Who is outside? Tell me!'

'No one, sir,' said Barrymore.

'Tell me,' said Sir Henry, 'or you shall leave this house

tomorrow. Tell me now!'

'Sir Henry,' said another voice, 'please don't be angry with my husband. It is my fault.'

We turned and saw Mrs Barrymore. She was standing at the top of the stairs, holding her hands tightly together.

'My brother is outside, sir,' she said. 'My brother is Selden, the man who escaped from prison.'

'Selden – the murderer?' I said. 'And why do you signal to him at night?'

'My husband takes him food and clothes,' said Mrs Barrymore. 'We signal to tell him my husband is coming.'

'I understand,' said Sir Henry. 'He is your brother; you must try to help him. Go to your room. We will talk about this in the morning.'

The Barrymores left the room.

Sir Henry turned and spoke to me. 'I am sorry for them, but Selden is a murderer. I must try to catch him.'

'Look!' I said. 'Look out of the window. There is a light on the moor.'

Sir Henry looked. A small light was shining on the moor. It was near High Tor.

'That's him!' said Sir Henry. 'Come, Dr Watson, we will go to that light. Bring your revolver.'

We put on our coats quickly and went out onto the moor. The moon was bright and so we could see the path across the moor. Also, we could see the signal light. It was about a mile away.

'There!' said Sir Henry. 'Selden is there. Hurry!'

I followed Sir Henry along the path across the moor. I was worried. I did not want Sir Henry to go far on the moor at night.

'Sir Henry,' said Mrs Barrymore, 'please don't be angry
with my husband. It is my fault.'

At that moment, we heard a strange sound. It was a deep howling sound. It came from some distance away.

'What's that?' asked Sir Henry. There was fear in his voice.

I was afraid too. 'It sounds like a dog,' I said. 'It sounds like a very large dog. Shall we turn back?'

'No,' said Sir Henry. 'We are nearly there. Look!'

In front of us, we saw the signal light clearly. It came from a lamp which stood on a rock. Beside the rock was a man, but the man did not see us. He was looking in the other direction.

Again we heard that deep howling sound – the sound of a huge dog. The sound was much nearer now. We heard the sound again. It was coming nearer all the time! The man by the rock heard the sound as well. He picked up the lantern and jumped on the rock. He looked one way, then the other. Suddenly he jumped off the rock and started to run.

He ran towards High Tor. He was running away from us. But he was not running away because he saw us. He was running away from something else which we could not see.

'Quick, Dr Watson, follow him!' shouted Sir Henry. 'Get your revolver ready.'

We ran along the narrow path. Near us, we heard the deep howling sound. It was very near and very loud. Then we heard a scream. We stopped.

'Be careful, Dr Watson,' said Sir Henry. 'Let us go forward slowly.'

The night was silent. We walked forward slowly. There was something, or someone, lying near the bottom of the Tor. We went over to it. I held my revolver in front of me.

We found the body of a man at the foot of the Tor.

We found the body of a man at the foot of the Tor.

The man had fallen from the rocky hill. He was dead. His neck was broken.

We were sure that the man was Selden. He was dressed in Sir Henry's old clothes – the clothes that Sir Henry had given to Barrymore.

I have one last strange thing to tell you, Holmes.

I looked up at the Tor from which Selden had fallen. Up above, at the top of the Tor, stood a tall, thin man. I saw him only for a moment. Then he disappeared into the night. But I know I have seen him before. I will search for this strange man who walks on the moor at night.

10

The Man On The Moor

Who was the man I had seen on High Tor? Was it the man Holmes and I had seen in London? But I was sure that the man on High Tor did not have a beard. Sir Henry did not see the man on the Tor and I said nothing to him.

There was nothing we could do for Selden. We went back to the house. What had Selden run away from? What had he seen? What had we heard? Was it the Hound of the Baskervilles? I felt safer in Baskerville Hall than out on the moor at night. Sir Henry felt the same.

In the morning, we sent for the police. They took Selden's body away.

Sir Henry told the Barrymores what had happened. But he did not speak about the strange sounds we had heard. Mrs Barrymore cried and covered her face with a handkerchief. Mr Barrymore said, 'It had to end. Poor Selden could not have lived on the moor in winter. It is far too cold.'

'Please forget what I said last night,' Sir Henry told them. 'I want you to stay at Baskerville Hall.'

'Thank you, sir. We will,' said Barrymore.

I went to my room and wrote a long report to Sherlock Holmes. Then I decided to go for a walk, but I did not want to walk on the moor. I did not like the moor.

Usually, I posted my letters to Holmes in Grimpen Village. But today I decided to walk to Coombe Tracey, the village to the south. It took me an hour to walk there along the road. On the way, I saw Stapleton.

'I heard you caught the escaped murderer,' said Stapleton. 'I will look forward to hearing the story from Sir Henry at dinner tomorrow.'

'Sir Henry is looking forward to dining with you and your sister tomorrow,' I replied.

'And so is my sister,' Stapleton said coldly. 'I look forward to seeing Sir Henry tomorrow at eight o'clock.'

'I will tell him,' I said. 'Good day.'

I walked on to Coombe Tracey and posted my letter. I saw a large house outside the village and asked who lived there.

'That is Mr Frankland's house,' the village shopkeeper told me.

Dr Mortimer had told me about Mr Frankland – and about Mr Frankland's interest in the stars. I decided to visit the gentleman and ask to see his telescope.

Mr Frankland was standing by his garden gate. He was a red-faced, elderly man with white hair.

'Good day,' I said, 'my name is Watson.'

'Dr Watson?' asked Mr Frankland.

'Yes,' I replied.

'I heard that you caught Selden last night on the moor,' said Mr Frankland. 'I nearly caught him myself.'

'How did you do that?' I asked in surprise.

'With my telescope. Come and see.'

Mr Frankland showed me into his house. I was very interested in his telescope. It was very large and powerful.

'I saw a man on the moor a number of times,' said Mr Frankland.

'Why did you not tell the police?' I asked.

'I was not sure that it was the murderer,' he replied. 'I began to think that perhaps there were two men on the moor. But why would anyone want to live out on the moor? There is no food and the weather is cold. Then, yesterday, I saw something.'

'What did you see?' I asked.

'I saw someone taking food out on the moor,' answered Mr Frankland.

'At night?' I asked. I thought of Barrymore and his signal light. Perhaps Mr Frankland had seen Barrymore taking food and clothing out to Selden.

'No,' said Mr Frankland. 'I saw a boy taking food during the day – and letters.'

'Letters?' I asked. 'Are you sure?'

'Very sure,' said Mr Frankland, 'because I know the boy. I asked the postman and learnt that the boy collects letters every day.'

'And where does he take them?' I asked.

'Look through the telescope,' said Mr Frankland. 'Look at that old farmhouse to the right of High Tor. That is High Tor Farm. Someone lives there, but I do not know who. He is a stranger.'

I looked through the telescope at High Tor. On the left of the Tor I saw the roof of Merripit House, where the Stapletons lived. On the right, I saw an old farmhouse. The roof was broken and so was one wall. But I saw smoke coming from the chimney.

'Thank you, Mr Frankland,' I said. 'Whoever lives there is not Selden. Selden is dead.'

I said goodbye to Mr Frankland. Then I decided to walk across the moor and look at old High Tor Farm. It was a mile or two away and I reached it late in the afternoon. The sun was low in the sky and the air was cold.

I walked up to the farmhouse slowly. The door was

'Someone lives there, but I do not know who. He is a stranger.'

broken and I looked inside. The farmhouse was empty and silent.

Part of the farmhouse was dry, where the roof was not broken. There was a wood fire on the floor and a bed in the corner. A lamp stood on a table with a pile of papers next to it.

I went into the farmhouse carefully. I put my hand into my jacket pocket where I kept my army revolver. I walked slowly to the table and looked at the pile of papers. I saw one of my own letters. Someone had stolen one of my own letters!

Who lived in the farmhouse? Was it the man with the black beard? Was it the man I had seen on the Tor?

I soon found out, as I heard the sound of footsteps outside. I took my revolver out of my pocket and turned towards the door. A tall, thin man stood in the doorway with his back to the setting sun. I could not see his face.

'It is a lovely evening, isn't it Watson?' the man said.

The man was Sherlock Holmes.

11

High Tor Farm

'Holmes!' I said in surprise. 'What are you doing here?'

'I am watching,' said Holmes. 'I am waiting for the murderer to show himself.'

'The murderer? Do you mean Selden? Selden is dead.'

'I know. I was on the Tor last night and saw what happened,' Holmes said. 'Someone wanted to kill Sir Henry Baskerville, not Selden.'

'But how long have you been here?' I asked. 'And why are you here in secret?'

'I came here on the same day as you,' answered Sherlock Holmes. 'I came in secret because the murderer is clever. He will not show himself if he knows I am here.'

'And what about my letters?' I asked. 'Have you read them?'

'Yes, I have,' Holmes replied. 'They were sent to me from London. But I have not read your report of last night. Come. Tell me about it as we walk to Baskerville Hall.

He left the farmhouse and I walked quickly after him. The sun had gone down and it was getting dark. A thick white mist was rising from the moor.

'You are a good detective,' said Holmes. 'Tell me, how did you find me? How did you know I was at High Tor Farm?'

'I did not know it was you,' I answered. 'Mr Frankland saw you through his telescope. And he saw the boy who brought you food and letters. He thought you were Selden, the murderer. Also, I saw you last night on the Tor.'

'I see,' said Holmes. 'If you saw me, I think the murderer of Sir Charles Baskerville saw me too. He will want to kill me as well as Sir Henry.'

'So,' I said, 'you think that Sir Charles was murdered?'

'I am sure of it,' said Holmes. 'Now, stay on the path.'

It was dark and the moon had not come up. We had to walk carefully. The path went through the Great Grimpen Mire and a sea of soft mud lay under the grass on either side of us.

Behind us, we heard that strange sound, the deep howling sound I had heard on the moor last night. It made me shiver with fear.

'What is it, Holmes?' I asked. 'Do you know what makes that sound.'

'No,' he answered, 'but the village people say it is the Hound of the Baskervilles. I will not go back to High Tor Farm tonight. Come. We must hurry. Keep your revolver ready.'

We walked quickly along the dark path. I was pleased to see the lights of Baskerville Hall in front of us. I was afraid of what was behind us – out on the moor, at night.

12

Setting the Trap

'Mr Sherlock Holmes,' said Sir Henry Baskerville, 'what a surprise! Welcome to Baskerville Hall.'

'Thank you,' said Holmes. 'But you did not obey my orders. Last night you went out on the moor. You were nearly murdered!'

'But I did not go alone,' said Sir Henry. 'Dr Watson was with me. He has a revolver to protect me.'

'And I shall protect you too,' said Holmes. 'Next time you go out on the moor at night, both Dr Watson and I will go with you.'

'The next time . . .' Sir Henry began.

'The next time will be tomorrow night,' said Holmes. 'Dr Watson tells me that you are going to dinner at Merripit House on the moor. I believe the Stapletons have invited you.'

'Yes,' Sir Henry said. 'And has Dr Watson told you that I want to marry Miss Stapleton?'

'Yes, he has,' said Holmes. 'Now I would like to ask Barrymore some questions.'

Sir Henry called for his servant, Barrymore. Barrymore came and stood in front of us. Sherlock Holmes looked at him carefully. Was this the man with the black beard we had seen in London?

'Tell me about Sir Charles Baskerville,' Holmes said to Barrymore. 'Did he often go for a walk at night?'

'No, sir,' said Barrymore, 'Sir Charles did not often leave the house at night.'

'But, on the night he died, he went for a walk on the edge of the moor,' said Holmes. 'We know he stood by the gate on the edge of the moor for about ten minutes. Was he waiting for someone?'

'I'm not sure, sir,' said Barrymore. 'I remember that Sir Charles received a letter that day.'

'A letter?' Holmes asked. 'Why do you remember this letter? Did you read it?'

'No, sir,' Barrymore said. 'I never read Sir Charles' letters. But Sir Charles usually kept his letters on his desk. This letter was unusual. He read it. Then he put it on the fire.'

'Oh, so he burnt it,' Holmes said. 'Perhaps this letter asked him to meet someone. Perhaps he went to this meeting and met someone – or something.'

'But why did Sir Charles burn the letter?' I asked.

'Why do people burn letters, Watson?' asked Holmes. 'Often because they have something to hide. But Sir Charles was afraid to go out on the moor at night. Dr Mortimer told us that Sir Charles believed the story of the

Hound of the Baskervilles. Why would he go out on the moor, alone, at night? If he was going to meet someone, it was someone he knew. But why meet on the edge of the moor? Was it a secret meeting?'

'Do you think Sir Charles was murdered by a friend?' I asked.

'I think he knew his murderer,' replied Holmes. 'And I think his murderer is not far away.'

After dinner, we sat in the library. There were paintings of the Baskerville family hanging on the walls. Some of the paintings were very old.

Sherlock Holmes looked at the paintings carefully. He was interested in the painting of Sir Hugo Baskerville, dated 1645.

'Interesting, Watson, very interesting,' said Holmes. 'Here is a painting of Sir Hugo, the man who started the story of the Hound of the Baskervilles. I am able to remember faces. Look at this black beard and the face. Have you seen this face before?'

'Yes, Holmes,' I said. 'It is the face of the man we saw in London. It is the man who followed Sir Henry in a cab!'

Sherlock Holmes was interested in the painting of
Sir Hugo Baskerville, dated 1645.

13

The Hound of the Baskervilles

Holmes got up early the next morning. He went to Grimpen Village and sent a telegram. When he returned to Baskerville Hall he was excited. 'We shall go hunting tonight,' he said, 'and Inspector Lestrade from Scotland Yard will come with us.'

'Why are we waiting until tonight?' I asked. 'You know who the murderer is, Holmes. Why can't we catch him before tonight?'

'We must make sure we have the right man,' Holmes said. 'We must wait. We will catch him tonight!'

Inspector Lestrade arrived from London at five o'clock. We met him at Grimpen Station. He was a short man, with bright eyes. He and Sherlock Holmes were good friends. He and Holmes talked together as we drove to Baskerville Hall.

At half past seven, when Sir Henry left the Hall, we were ready.

Sir Henry walked along the path across the Great Grimpen Mire, towards Merripit House. The Stapletons had asked him to come to dinner at eight o'clock.

The three of us followed him – Lestrade, Holmes and I. Each of us carried a revolver. We saw Sir Henry go into Merripit House. We waited below High Tor, about two hundred yards from the house.

The lights burned brightly in Merripit House and the curtains of the dining room were open. We saw Sir Henry talking to Stapleton.

'Where is Miss Stapleton?' I said to Holmes. 'Sir Henry has come to see her, not her brother.'

'Perhaps Stapleton wants to talk to Sir Henry alone,' Holmes said. 'But, look – the mist is rising. Soon we will not be able to see.'

I looked around. Thick white mist was rising from the Great Grimpen Mire.

'Shall we climb up the Tor?' I asked. 'Perhaps we will be able to see better from above the mist.'

We climbed a little way up the Tor. But the mist was so thick we could see only a few yards in front of us.

'I did not think of this,' said Holmes. 'Our plan may fail if we cannot see clearly. We must listen for any sounds from Merripit House.'

We waited in the mist and the moon came up. The white moonlight shone through the mist, but we could not see Merripit House or the path across the moor.

We listened. At last we heard a door open, then the sound of voices. Stapleton was saying goodnight to Sir Henry. Then we heard footsteps below the Tor. Someone was walking along a stony part of the path.

At the same time, we heard another sound. It was the sound of a metal chain and came from Merripit House. Then we heard the deep howling sound of a huge dog.

'The Hound!' Holmes shouted. 'Sir Henry! Sir Henry! Climb the Tor! We are here on the Tor! Hurry!'

Lestrade moved forward to help Sir Henry. But we could not see clearly in the mist.

'Keep back!' Holmes shouted to Lestrade.

Lestrade cried out and fired his revolver into the mist. We saw the yellow flash of the revolver and we heard the loud bang. 'It's coming!' Lestrade cried out. He fired again.

In the light of the flash, we saw a huge black shape.

In the light of the flash, we saw a huge black shape.

Its eyes and jaws were burning bright with fire. It was a horrible huge monster. It ran past Lestrade. We heard Sir Henry cry out.

We heard the sound of falling stones.

Holmes and I both fired our revolvers at the black shape. We heard a howl. We fired again and again. Then we moved forward carefully and climbed down the Tor.

Sir Henry was at the bottom of the Tor. He had fallen, but he was not hurt. He now stood up carefully.

'What was it, Mr Holmes?' he asked. 'What was that thing in the mist?'

Holmes walked along the path, reloading his revolver with bullets. 'We are safe,' he called back. 'The dog is dead.'

I went to look. There on the path lay the largest black dog I have ever seen. Fire burned around the dog's eyes and mouth. Blood was pouring from its head.

'Could it have killed Sir Henry?' I asked.

'It would have frightened him,' said Holmes. 'The path across the Great Grimpen Mire is narrow. If he had run in the dark, Sir Henry would have fallen into the mire and died.'

'But where did it come from?' I asked. 'And why is its head burning with fire?'

'I believe it was kept in Merripit House,' said Holmes. 'The fire is easy to explain.'

He touched the dog's head with his fingers. 'It is a special paint,' he said. 'Come. Let us find the murderer.'

We walked back to Merripit House. The door was open. Sir Henry went into the house. 'Miss Stapleton!' he shouted. 'Where is she? She did not join us for dinner.'

A sound came from one of the rooms. Sir Henry pushed

the door open. Miss Stapleton lay on the bed. Her hands and feet were tied together. There was a cloth tied across her mouth.

Sir Henry cut the rope around her hands. Holmes took the cloth from her mouth.

'Where is your brother, Miss Stapleton?' Sir Henry asked.

Miss Stapleton looked at the floor. 'Gone,' she said. 'My husband has gone.'

'Your husband!' shouted Sir Henry. 'You are Mrs Stapleton?'

'Yes, I am his wife,' she said. 'But his name is not Stapleton. He is the son of your dead uncle, Roger Baskerville. He is your cousin.'

Out on the moor we heard a terrible cry. We ran outside. The mist was thick on the Great Grimpen Mire. The cry came again, and then a loud scream. Then silence.

'I believe that the Great Grimpen Mire has taken your cousin,' Holmes said to Sir Henry. 'He has fallen into the mire. We shall never find his body.'

14

Back In Baker Street

'There are still some things I don't understand,' I said to Holmes. 'Tell me – who was Stapleton? Why did he want to kill Sir Henry?'

'It is simple, my dear Watson,' said Holmes. 'Remember Sir Charles had two brothers. The youngest brother, Roger, was a bad man. He got into trouble over money and went to

South America. He died in Venezuela. He did not marry, so no one knew he had a son.'

'And this son called himself Stapleton?'

'Yes, and the son was both bad and clever. He wanted the Baskerville money. There were only two Baskervilles left alive – Sir Charles and Sir Henry. If they died, Baskerville Hall would belong to Stapleton.'

'What about his wife? Why did Stapleton say she was his sister?'

'At first, Stapleton wanted her to marry Sir Charles or Sir Henry. That was a way of getting the money.'

'What an evil man!' I said. 'But she did not want to help Stapleton. She tried to warn both of them, didn't she?'

'Yes, she tried to meet Sir Charles the night he died. But Stapleton found out. Stapleton waited for Sir Charles and frightened him to death with the black dog. Also, Mrs Stapleton sent the note to Sir Henry at the Northumberland Hotel. Then Sir Henry fell in love with Mrs Stapleton, so Stapleton was worried and angry. At last, Stapleton had to tie her up to stop her telling Sir Henry.'

'And Stapleton was the man with the black beard?'

'Yes, he tried to hide his face. He put on a beard when he followed Sir Henry in London.'

'What about the missing boots?' I asked.

'The dog and the boots go together,' Holmes said. 'Stapleton knew the silly story about the Hound of the Baskervilles. And he knew that Sir Charles believed the story. So, Stapleton bought that huge black dog and let it walk on the moor at night.'

'But the boots,' I said. 'What about the stolen boots?'

'Watson, you are very slow,' said Holmes. 'It was a hunting dog. Hunting dogs will follow a smell. Stapleton wanted some of Sir Henry's clothes to give to the dog. He paid a waiter at the hotel to steal the boots. But the first boot did not work because it was new. It did not have Sir Henry's smell. Then, remember, the dog hunted Selden because Selden was wearing Sir Henry's old clothes.'

'What a strange story,' I said. 'Stapleton was clever.'

'Yes, my dear Watson,' said Holmes. 'I needed your help to catch him. Now, why don't you write about it? Perhaps you can call your story *The Case of the Stolen Boot*?'

POINTS
FOR
UNDERSTANDING

Points For Understanding

1

1 Who is telling this story?
2 What is Sherlock Holmes' address?
3 Why had Dr Mortimer come to visit Holmes?

2

1 Where does Dr Mortimer live?
2 Who was Sir Charles Baskerville?
3 What had happened to Sir Charles?
4 Tell the story of the Curse of the Hound of the Baskervilles.
5 Did Sherlock Holmes believe this story?
6 Where had Dr Mortimer found Sir Charles' body?
7 Dr Mortimer found many footprints on the ground.
   How had these footprints been made?

3

1 What had happened to the footprints?
2 How did Dr Mortimer know Sir Charles had waited by the
   wooden gate?
3 Dr Mortimer is meeting Sir Henry Baskerville.
       (a) Who is he?
       (b) Where is he meeting him?
       (c) Where has he been living?
4 Where did Sherlock Holmes tell Dr Mortimer to stay that
   night?
5 What did Sherlock Holmes tell Dr Mortimer to do the next
   day?
6 'There are three questions,' said Holmes. What are the three
   questions?

4

1 How old was Sir Henry? What did he look like?
2 Sir Henry had received a letter that morning. Describe the letter and say why it was unusual.
3 What strange thing had happened when Sir Henry was in his hotel bedroom?
4 'Quick, Watson, we must follow him.'
   (a) Who did Holmes and Watson follow?
   (b) Why did they follow him?
5 Who sent the letter to Sir Henry Baskerville?

5

1 Why was Sir Henry angry at lunch?
2 Why did Holmes think it was safer for Sir Henry to go to Dartmoor than to stay in London?
3 Holmes wanted someone to go with Sir Henry to Baskerville Hall. Who was this?
4 Who will become the owner of Baskerville Hall if Sir Henry dies?
5 How much money did Sir Henry have?

6

1 Holmes told Watson to stay near to Sir Henry.
   (a) What must Sir Henry not do at night?
   (b) What had Watson brought with him?
2 On the way to Baskerville Hall, Watson saw a soldier guarding the road. Why was the soldier guarding the road?
3 Why did Watson want to go back to London?
4 Why did Dr Mortimer leave Sir Henry and Watson?
5 'I am Barrymore,' said the man.
   (a) Who was Barrymore?
   (b) Describe Barrymore.
   (c) Did Watson think he had seen Barrymore before?
6 What did Watson hear at night while he was writing a letter to Holmes?

7

1   Who did Stapleton say he lived with?
2   What happened to anyone who fell in the Great Grimpen Mire?
3   As Watson and Stapleton were walking to Stapleton's house, they heard a strange sound.
    (a)   What did Watson say made the sound?
    (b)   What did Stapleton say made the sound?
4   Describe Miss Stapleton. Did Watson think she looked like her brother?
5   Miss Stapleton walked outside with Dr Watson.
    (a) What did she tell him had made the strange sound?
    (b)   What did she tell Watson to do?

8

1   What did Sir Charles do while he stood by the gate?
2   Dr Mortimer told Dr Watson about Mr Frankland.
    (a) Where does Mr Frankland live?
    (b) What does Mr Frankland use to look at the stars?
    (c) Why is Mr Frankland looking at the moor?
3   Who has Sir Henry become good friends with?
4   What question did Sir Henry ask Barrymore? What was Barrymore's reply?
5   What did Sir Henry give Barrymore?
6   What did Dr Watson see in the middle of the night?

9

1   What has Dr Watson found out about Sir Henry?
2   Sir Henry went out onto the moor alone. What did Dr Watson do?
3   What did Sir Henry tell Dr Watson about Stapleton?
4   Who was Barrymore signalling to out on the moor? Why was he sending a signal?
5   Why did Sir Henry and Dr Watson go out onto the moor?
6   What strange sound did they hear?
7   What did Watson and Sir Henry find lying near the bottom of the Tor?
8   What did Dr Watson see for a moment at the top of the Tor?

10

1   Describe the man Dr Watson had seen on top of the Tor.
2   'I saw a man on the moor a number of times,' said Mr
    Frankland.
    (a)   Why did Mr Frankland not tell the police?
    (b)   How many men did Mr Frankland begin to think
          were on the moor?
3   What was the boy taking out on the moor during the day?
4   Where was the boy taking the letters to?
5   Who was the other man on the moor?

11

1   When did Holmes come to Dartmoor?
2   Which other person will the murderer of Sir Henry want to
    murder?
3   Why was Dr Watson pleased to see the lights of Baskerville
    Hall?

12

1   'The next time . . .' Sir Henry began.
    (a)   When was Sir Henry going out on the moor again?
    (b)   Who was going with him?
    (c)   Who was Sir Henry going to visit?
2   Barrymore told Holmes that Sir Charles had received a letter
    on the day he died.
    (a)   What did Sir Charles do after he read the letter?
    (b)   What did Holmes think was in the letter?
3   Dr Watson asks, 'Do you think Sir Charles was murdered by
    a friend?' What was Holmes' reply?
4   Holmes pointed to a painting of Sir Hugo Baskerville. What
    did Holmes think was interesting about the painting?

13

1   Who did Holmes invite to come and join them at Baskerville
    Hall?

2   Sir Henry walked across the path to Merripit House.
    (a) Who followed behind him?
    (b) What did they each carry?
    (c) Where did Sir Henry go?
    (d) Where did the three wait?
3   Why was Holmes afraid their plan might fail?
4   What sound did they hear coming from Merripit House?
5   Lestrade fired his gun. Describe what they saw in the light of
    the flash.
6   What had been killed? How had its face been made to burn
    with fire?
7   Who was 'Miss Stapleton'?
8   What happened to Stapleton?

14

1   Explain who Stapleton was.
2   Why did Stapleton want his wife to marry Sir Henry?
3   Why had Stapleton's wife tried to warn Sir Charles?
4   How had Sir Charles died?
5   Who was the man with the black beard?
6   Explain why two of Sir Henry's boots had been stolen from
    his hotel in London.
7   Why had the dog hunted the murderer, Selden?

ELEMENTARY LEVEL

Road to Nowhere *by John Milne*
The Black Cat *by John Milne*
Don't Tell Me What To Do *by Michael Hardcastle*
The Runaways *by Victor Canning*
The Red Pony *by John Steinbeck*
The Goalkeeper's Revenge and Other Stories *by Bill Naughton*
The Stranger *by Norman Whitney*
The Promise *by R. L. Scott-Buccleuch*
The Man With No Name *by Evelyn Davies and Peter Town*
The Cleverest Person in the World *by Norman Whitney*
Claws *by John Landon*
Z for Zachariah *by Robert C. O'Brien*
Tales of Horror *by Bram Stoker*
Frankenstein *by Mary Shelley*
Silver Blaze and Other Stories *by Sir Arthur Conan Doyle*
Tales of Ten Worlds *by Arthur C. Clarke*
The Boy Who Was Afraid *by Armstrong Sperry*
Room 13 and Other Ghost Stories *by M. R. James*
The Narrow Path *by Francis Selormey*
The Woman in Black *by Susan Hill*

For further information on the full selection of
Readers at all five levels in the series, please refer
to the Macmillan Guided Readers catalogue.

Published by Macmillan Heinemann ELT
Between Towns Road, Oxford OX4 3PP
Macmillan Heinemann ELT is an imprint of
Macmillan Publishers Limited
Companies and representatives throughout the world

ISBN 0 435 27140 7

This retold version by Stephen Colbourn for Macmillan Guided Readers
First published 1992
Design and illustration © Macmillan Publishers Limited 2002
Heinemann is a registered trademark of Reed Educational & Professional Publishing Limited
This version first published 2002

Illustrated by Kay Dixey
Cover by Nick Hardcastle and Threefold Design

Printed in Thailand

2008 2007 2006 2005 2004 2003
20 19 18 17 16 15 14 13 12